My Brother
Ange

My Brother Ange

Ange

by Mary McCaffrey

illustrations
by Denise Saldutti

THOMAS Y. CROWELL   New York

Fields Corner

Text copyright © 1982 by Mary McCaffrey
Illustrations copyright © 1982 by Denise Saldutti
All rights reserved. Printed in the United States of America. No part of this book
may be used or reproduced in any manner whatsoever without written permission except
in the case of brief quotations embodied in critical articles and reviews. For information
address Thomas Y. Crowell Junior Books, 10 East 53rd Street, New York, N.Y. 10022.
Designed by Joyce Hopkins

Library of Congress Cataloging in Publication Data

McCaffrey, Mary.
My brother Ange.
"Originally published in Great Britain as Smokedrift to heaven"—Verso t.p.
    SUMMARY: When eleven-year-old Mick's little brother is hit by a car after the two
boys fight, Mick is filled with remorse and vows to be good to him in the future.
    [1. Brothers and sisters—Fiction] I. Saldutti, Denise, ill. II. Title.
PZ7.M122836My 1982   [Fic]   81–43887
                                AACR2
ISBN 0–690–04194–2 ISBN 0–690–04195–0 (lib. bdg.)

1 2 3 4 5 6 7 8 9 10

First Edition

To my son
Victor Alexander Szudek
and P.P. who knew about it first

Contents

My Brother Ange

1

"Don't Forget the Olive Oil!"

Mick Tooley stood the jar of clean paintbrushes on the drainboard, tugged at the roller towel, and dried his hands on a clean place.

"Thank you, Michael. You've been a great help, as always," his teacher said, settling down to mark a pile of papers.

Mr. Rivers never dashed off to the staff room for a quick smoke, or to get the first bus home. No matter how long Mick stayed behind doing little jobs in the classroom, Mr. Rivers was always there working.

"Shall I water the plants, sir?" asked Mick.

"Done, thanks," replied Mr. Rivers.

"The board, I could clean it a bit better. Maybe wash it if—"

"Not to worry, Michael. Don't forget, your brother's waiting. Off you go, now." Mr. Rivers looked over his glasses, pointed to the door, and smiled. "Good night. See you on Monday."

"But, can I just—? Well, good night, sir."

Mick picked up his bookbag, slowly slung it over his shoulder, and, with a backward glance at his teacher, went out and trotted down the flight of stairs to the playground. He shaded his eyes from the orange November sun and scanned the swirling mass of children in the yard.

The setting sun silhouetted a thin, impish figure swinging around the signpost by the main gate. Mick's young brother Angelo was waiting for him.

SAINT JOHN'S Primary School
Downhill Road. London SW2

said the sign over the imp.

Mick was eleven, in his last year at primary school. His brother was seven. As Mick reached the gate, Angelo's ruler and pencil case fell from his bouncing bookbag. Mick stooped to pick them up. "Come on, Ange," he said. "Let's go."

"Olive oil! Don't forget the olive oil, Mick. Mama wants olive oil," panted Angelo. His spindly

4

legs coming to a stop. "Not peanut, not sunflower, not corn—"

"I know, I know! Here, take these and fasten your bag," said Mick irritably. He often felt irritable with his brother, and wished he wasn't always with him. He checked that Ange's bag was fastened and strode out of the gate.

"Hold on, Mick," someone called. "I'm going your way."

It was Napoleon Leroy, his classmate. The one with the biggest feet in the school, and a heart to match. Everyone called him Leon, for short.

"Why? Have you moved?" asked Mick.

"No, man. Going to my uncle's. He's fixing my bike. If you ever need your bike fixed, Uncle Sam's your man. Ain't nothing he can't do with bikes."

"That's great," said Mick. He didn't add that he had no bike. He'd never had a bike.

"It's an International Super—luminous green. Folds up for easy storage in the car, you know," Leon added. "Trouble is, it folds up when I'm on it, so my uncle's going to fix it so it stays put. Hiya, Ange!"

"Hiya, Nappy! How'd you like the Isle of Wight?"*

Leon had been one of the lucky ones from the

* Island in the English Channel, off the coast of southern England.

two top classes who had gone on a school trip with a couple of the teachers. Mick hadn't put his name in to go. They never went on trips. Their mother couldn't afford it.

"You cut out the Nappy, squirt," Leon said good-humoredly. "The Isle of Wight was okay, except it rained. Ten days of rain, man, and no ark! That reminds me. Have you ever seen one of these?"

Leon pulled a pencil from his pocket. It seemed ordinary enough, but fastened onto the tip of it was a plastic tube filled with colored stripes.

"What's in the tube?" asked Mick.

"Guess."

"I can't. Grains of something?"

"Yeah, sand. That's the different colors you can find on the Isle of Wight. Neat, isn't it?"

"Terrific. I've never seen one of these before. It's too nice to use," Mick said admiringly.

"Don't you worry. I won't *use* it," said Leon. "I just brought it in to show. Tell you what, I've got another one at home. You can have that one."

"I can! What for?"

"What for? For nothing! For, because I want you to have it, that's all. I'll bring it on Monday. See you, pal." And Leon was gone, loping across the road to the apartments where his uncle lived.

The apartments were fairly new, block after block of them, with overhead walkways to link the build-

6

ings like a maze, or maybe a prison. Underneath, all the garages had had their windows smashed; the holes gaped black like blinded eyes. The people who had no garage space kept their cars in the street, bumper to bumper. It was dangerous to walk to and from school this way. There was no sidewalk, only space for cars. You had to walk along the narrow road between the lines of parked cars, and scramble out of the way if someone came driving along. Maybe somebody needed statistics, thought Mick, like, "At least two children in every class killed and half a dozen injured—we must make the area safe!"

"Always walk home with Angelo," Mama said regularly. "Remember, Mick, Angelo is never *ever* to walk past those apartments by himself. They're death traps for children. He's got to wait for you every day. I'm relying on you, Mick." Mick knew the whole speech by heart.

"D'you like Napoleon?" asked Angelo, bobbing about at Mick's side.

" 'Course I do."

They took the shortcut across the park instead of the High Street, and had almost reached home when Mick realized he had forgotten something.

"Oh, no!" he moaned. "I didn't get the olive oil."

"Oh, Mick! I can't walk all the way back to the

store," cried Angelo. "I'm tired. Can't I go home and wait—please?" He dropped his bookbag from his shoulder and scuffed his shoes along the pavement.

"Nope! You've got to stay with me. Mama says so. It was Leon made me forget. Come on, it won't take long."

"But I'll miss *Jackanory** on television."

"No, you won't. Shut up!"

"Que-e-e-e-eh!" replied Angelo, crinkling his eyes tightly shut and showing his white teeth and two gaps. The long-drawn-out noise he made was a cross between a duck's quack and the sound of an automobile horn.

---

* An English television program similar to Sesame Street.

2

Empty Chairs

Mick and Angelo climbed the stairs of the crumbling old house in Nightingale Rise—with the olive oil. As they reached the brown varnished door on the third floor, Mick took the key from his blazer pocket. His breath came more slowly now, and more heavily, as he fitted the key into the lock.

They came home like this every day since Granny Mia had died. How they had loved their Italian grandmother. "We love you, Granny Mia!" they had squealed, climbing all over her. And she had smiled, her dark old eyes like burning coals, and had offered her soft arms that hardly went around two boys at the same time.

She had often said to Mick, "You are the first-a man in your-a family. Look after your-a Ma-ma." Just as Mama now said, "Look after Angelo." It was a kind of chain of looking-afters.

Granny Mia had always been caring and loving and giving. But then suddenly Granny Mia's plumpness wasn't there anymore. The skin on her arms hung loosely, in folds, as though it was a size too big for her. Her clothes looked too big for her, until the day came when she wasn't there at all.

Mick didn't remember much about the funeral, except for the big candles, their smoke drifting upward in the high vaulted church. "Look at the smoke drift," Ange had whispered. Smokedrift—like snowdrift, cloud drift, or spindrift. And there had been a coffin that had looked too modern and much too small for Granny Mia. Mama hadn't cried. She had just stared and stared. And she had stared for weeks afterward. They had all stared for years, it seemed, at the cane chair in the corner where Granny Mia had always sat with her knitting and crocheting. Yet it was only three months ago that she had died. . . .

Mick stared at the empty chair now, through the open door. The bright crocheted cushions were piled up on the seat as always. Mick remembered the Christmas before, when Ange had swiped the pink Italian bowl onto the floor during a game of blindman's bluff. It had been a kind of square lattice-work bowl with pictures of saints at the center on each side—the "holy bowly" they had called it. Granny Mia had been terribly upset when it was smashed. Mick couldn't get used to the corner without it, and *that* had been only a piece of porcelain. But the corner without Granny Mia! It was like part of somebody else's house.

She would never be there again. The newscaster would go on telling of murders, bombings, and kidnappings, and she wouldn't be there to cross herself, sigh, and mutter, "Santa Maria! Santa Maria!" Mick willed her to be there, day after day. If only he could open the door and see her sitting in her chair, as if she had never been away!

"Hurry up, Mick. I'm tired," complained Angelo, thrusting the door wide open with one foot. He dived in under Mick's arm.

"Stop behaving like a baby," said Mick.

"Que-e-e-eh!" retorted Angelo.

"D'you want to share a teabag? Remember, it's Mama's late night."

"Oh, I hate Fridays!" said Angelo. "Why does Mama have to be late on Fridays? Why does she? I'm starving."

"Because the shop's open late. You know very

well, and you're not the only one who's starving. I hardly had any lunch. That meat pie at school is foul. It's only good for smoke signals." Mick and Leon liked to lift up the crust of their pies and send S.O.S. signals to each other across the table.

Mick dropped his bookbag by the door and went into the kitchen with the olive oil. "I'll make us a peanut butter and jam sandwich. Okay?"

"Okay." Angelo was already tipping his box of toy cars onto the living room rug.

"Wash your hands, then," called Mick.

Angelo spat on each palm and rubbed his hands together. "Done!" he yelled.

"Ange? Wash!"

"Oh, all right!"

Mick cut the bread, badly, great wedges of it. He wished Mama would buy the sliced kind, but she never would. "Crusty bread's good for you, and it tastes better—*and* the crumbs can always be swept up," she would say before Mick could plead against the crumby mess it made.

Mick hated Fridays too. But he tried to hate them silently, so that Ange might get out of hating them. He didn't really like any nights now, with Mama rushing in hot and tired. But worst of all were the empty chairs.

The second one was pushed back against the wall. It was a chair Mick never sat in, and tried never to look at. But he knew it was there—an old arm-chair squeezed into a yellow stretch cover, to help keep its stuffing from falling out.

Mick carried the tea and sandwiches into the living room. "Here, Ange, take this. If you're a pig and spill any, you clean it up yourself, remember."

"I'm not a pig," replied Angelo, breathing into his tea mug. "Pig yourself."

They sat on the floor to have their snack. It took the sharpness off their hunger. In the old days, Granny Mia had met them at the school gate with something to eat, usually apples. And she had cooked dinner, so it was ready when Mama came in. Now they had to wait longer, and get something themselves if they felt hungry.

Mick switched on the television. They rolled onto their stomachs and watched a story about a boy who lived in a beautiful white house with a low white fence all around the lawn. Everything inside the house was bright and clean and shiny. It was full of the kind of things anybody would love to have.

Mick felt envious. That was the way to live. In a new, clean house with a yard, a fence, and plenty of space to have a dog, a cat, and a bicycle. The boy had a big bedroom crammed with books and models, and loads of space to do things on the floor. He didn't have to sleep in a cubbyhole with bunk beds. It certainly wasn't like Nightingale Rise.

"I think I'll live in a house like that when I grow up," Mick remarked as he collected the tea mugs. "With a German shepherd dog, and a swimming pool when I can afford it."

"Que-e-e-e-eh," said Angelo. "Yuck-yuck! Que-e-e-e-eh!"

"Oh, you drive me crazy with your stupid noise! How about being rich, Ange? Then Mama wouldn't have to go out to work anymore."

"Well, I'm going to college first, to get a degree in—you know what."

"No, what?"

"Que-e-e-e-eh! I'll do it in English! Que-e-e-e-eh! In Chinese! Que-e-e-e-eh! And of course in French! Que-e-e-e-eh!" He made the French sound by holding his nose. Then he made his ears move and dived under the table with a toy car.

"Shut up! You're just stupid," said Mick sourly. He went to the kitchen and rinsed the tea mugs under the cold tap, letting the water run on and on with his thoughts. How could he be expected to look after Ange? he wondered. How could *anybody* look after a brother who behaved like a loony duck?

He thought of Napoleon Leroy. There were six children in his family, boys and girls, and they talked to one another. He'd heard them. They actually

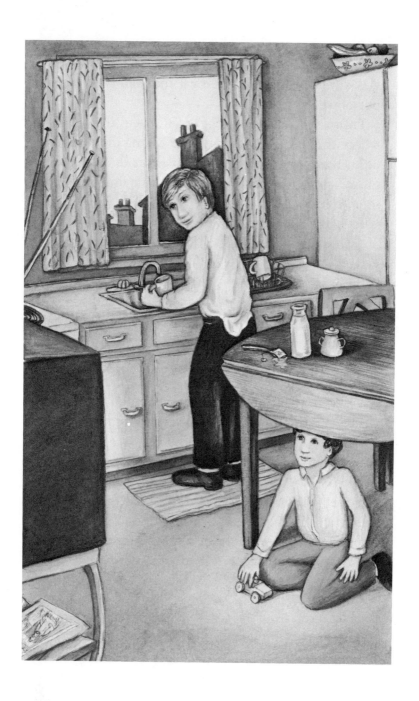

talked and played together. It was only Ange who was different. Mick turned off the water and went out onto the landing.

From the window they could see the corner where they would catch sight of Mama in the lamplight. She would wave to them in its deep sodium glow, and with that wave, life would immediately seem better.

At exactly a quarter to seven she came into view. She freed one hand from her shopping bags and waved.

"Mama's here, Ange," Mick called.

Angelo barged out onto the landing and lunged at the window. "Hooray! Mama! Yoo-hoo, Mama!" he shouted, as if she could hear him.

At once there was a knocking from below.

"Cut out the noise! Cut it out! I can't hear a thing on my TV!" Mr. Logie, who owned the house, peered up the stairs. "You kids are a menace. Now cut it out!"

Mick and Angelo tiptoed back. "Logie-the-bogey! Logie-the-bogey!" chanted Angelo in a voice that was well above a whisper.

Mick put a pot of water on to boil for the spaghetti, and a few minutes later Mama's footsteps could be heard on the threadbare stair-carpet.

3

Gray Roofs of Life

"Is your head bad, Mama?" Mick asked as his mother, sighing, heaved her bags onto the kitchen table.

"Pretty bad."

"The kettle's on. I'll get you a cup of tea." Mick reached for a teabag.

His mother's eyes rested fondly on him for a moment before she said, "Where's Angelo? He's not—"

"No such luck. He's around," Mick replied gruffly. His mother's look just had time to change to one of reproach before a "Que-e-e-eh!"

screamed in their ears. Angelo flew out of the cup-board under the sink, with the plastic bucket rolling out after him.

"You idiot!" shouted Mick angrily. "You'll kill somebody one of these days. Shocks can kill, you know!" In his heart he said, *But please, God, don't let it be Mama. She's all that's left.*

Angelo's wild hug brought the smile back to their mother's face. "Angelo! I hope you don't behave like this with your teacher," Mama said.

"Bet he does," said Mick, pressing the water out of the teabag with a spoon. "Mrs. Gentle's nearly mental and Ange'll put her in the nuthouse before long. Now Mr. Rivers, he's—"

"Mr. Rivers! Mr. Rivers! I'm fed up with hearing about Mr. Rivers," said Angelo, covering his ears with a dish towel. "You'd think he was the whole world, the way you go on. You and your Mr. Rivers!"

"He's better than your teacher any day, so shut up, spindle-shanks." Mick advanced on his brother, but Angelo did not reply. He looked steadily at Mick for a moment; then his lower lip began to quiver. He turned, ran out of the kitchen, and dived under the table again to join his cars.

Mama held her head for a moment, and then put the spaghetti into the boiling water. "Oh, my head, my head," she murmured. "I think it's the music that does it. It never stops all day."

The place where she worked had once been a department store. Now it was a kind of covered market that sold all sorts of things, including clothes, ornaments, rugs, and toys—even fruit and vegetables, but no other food. It was not what she really wanted, but it was the only job she could get.

"You know, they put on one record after another," she continued. "And they all sound the same to me. Oh—there's a job opening up at the Mini Market next month, or so I hear. I'd like that."

"Do you think you'll get it?" asked Mick.

"I don't know—we'll see. It would still mean late Fridays, but at least I'd get the shopping done."

"Wow! Free food! Steak, beans, and chips every night! Wagon-wheels, crisps* and chewing gum!" cried Angelo excitedly, peering out from under the table in the living room.

"No, it wouldn't be free," Mama said, smiling. "But things would be cheaper. I'd get a bit off everything." She was well on the way with dinner. The smell of minestrone soup was rising in the kitchen, with the scent of beef and bay leaves.

"Can we have dumplings, Mama? Please say yes. Pleasy! Pleasy!" Angelo crawled forward dramatically on his knees to the kitchen door. His soul

_____
* English crackers

19

seemed to peep out through his huge dark eyes when he wanted something. He could get around Mama for anything, Mick thought.

"What—*now*?" Mama asked hesitantly. She gulped her tea. "Well, I—I—"

"No! No!" interrupted Mick. "Mama's too tired. We're not having dumplings just for you. Why don't you stop thinking about yourself? Greedy-guts!" Exasperated, he pushed Angelo's shoulder.

At once, Angelo made the most of it and fell over backward onto the floor. "Ow! Ow! You hit me! You knocked me over! Ow! Ow!" he yelled. "You're rotten, Mick!"

"Mick, that wasn't very kind," said Mama. She hadn't seen exactly what had happened.

"But I only—I didn't—I only tried to—oh, what's the use!"

Mick suddenly felt sick in his throat. He flung himself out of the kitchen and rushed into his bedroom, slamming the door. The more he tried to take care of things, the worse they got. It wasn't enough to see to Ange's safety, to feed his hungry stomach, to help with the shopping, to make Mama's tea, to save Mama from Ange's endless demands. . . .

Mick looked at the dull gray roofs visible through the bedroom window. Life was like that—dull and gray, every day the same, and nothing exciting to look forward to, only taking care of Ange.

Mick stared at the roofs until they became blurred. It seemed like hours later when Mama called, "Mi-ick! Dinner's ready."

He went to the kitchen. Ange was already stuffing himself with dumplings. Mama had made dumplings after all, to please him. Spaghetti hung from Ange's mouth, twitching like live white worms, and the russet spaghetti sauce was spread around his mouth like greasepaint. He looked as if his next act would be clowning at the circus.

4

Another Long Saturday

Mick woke at eight o'clock on Saturday morning to find Angelo's toes dangling just above his head. He shut his eyes tightly to blot out the toes, and turned over to face the wall.

For a few moments, he dreamt of a super bedroom, like the one he had seen on television. He'd have his ceiling painted dark blue, and he'd stick large cutouts of planets on it and give them names like Trisphere, Hextoro, Octagonia. Then from his bed he would lie looking upward, floating in his own galaxy. He'd have a desk in his room, bookshelves, and two lamps. One lamp would be on

the desk and the other at his bedside. That would be real luxury—to lean over and flick off your own lamp when you'd finished reading, instead of getting out of bed to reach the wall switch.

Mick stretched out his left arm, pretending to turn off his lamp, but he was not allowed to dream for long. Angelo began rocking sideways on the top bunk. The bed creaked. It went on creaking.

"You'll break the bed, Ange. Stop it!" Mick shouted, rolling out of bed onto the floor. He couldn't sit up in bed because the metal links above tore at his hair. "And if it collapses, I'll be killed. *I'll* be the one in the sandwich."

"Oh yez! Oh yez! Fresh meat spread! Que-e-e-e-eh!" crowed Angelo. He jumped down to the floor with a thud and ran off toward the bathroom.

Mick picked up Ange's shirt and sweater from the floor and threw them after him. "You'd better clean up this room today. It's full of your junk. I could have a nice-looking place here if it wasn't for you!"

The shirt and sweater were just hitting the bathroom door when Mama appeared.

"It's *Saturday* again," she said dully. "Try to keep your temper with Angelo for once, Mick. Saturdays with you two are getting me down."

Mick looked at the floor, and began to pick up Angelo's clothes. He knew what Mama meant. The weekends were hard, but it was only when they were nearly over that he felt any remorse, and then it was too late. He knew they were lucky to have Mama at home on Saturdays. She was specially allowed to work just five days a week at the shop, because of their being on their own without Granny Mia. Weekends were like candy bars. Mama gave them each a candy bar on Saturdays after they had cleaned the apartment. Mick could almost die of hunger all week, longing for that candy. Then, when he'd gobbled it all at once, he'd wish he was just about to enjoy it all over again, slowly, bit by bit.

Mick raised his eyes and looked at Mama as she called to Ange through the bathroom door. She was wearing her jeans and sweater. He could tell which day of the week it was just by looking at her. Tomorrow, Sunday, she would be wearing high-heeled shoes and her red jersey dress, and a white beret with a brooch in it. But first they had to get through another long Saturday.

Mama did the washing early on Saturday. Two gray school uniforms were hanging on the clothesline outside the kitchen window by breakfast time. Then they cleaned the apartment together. After that, Mama gave all her time to the boys.

"What would you like to do today?" she would ask. And her generosity showed, the way she left herself wide open to suggestions.

24

"What would you like to do today?" she asked now.

Angelo was under the table with his felt-tip pens and a pad of paper, covering page after page with weird-looking creatures from his colorful imagination. He had taken to living under the table since Granny Mia had died, like a tortoise in a shell. "What about that bulletin board you promised us, Mama?" he asked in his high-pitched voice. "You said we could have one, and I've got tons of pictures to put up."

"Oh, that!" Mama looked doubtful. "I meant that for when we get another place. When we get a real home."

"Isn't this a real home?" Angelo held the ends of the tablecloth around his face, peeping out like an old woman in a kerchief.

"Well, it's only makeshift. One day we'll have a—a real house." Mama didn't sound too hopeful.

"What about a makeshift bulletin board, then?" Angelo persisted.

Mick finished sharpening his pencils and was about to protest, but a look from Mama stopped him. "What about it, Mick? If you give me a hand, maybe we could manage it between us."

"I don't know. It would be nice, but really we need . . ." His voice trailed away. He had nearly said "Dad"—a word he hadn't used in over a year.

He often thought about his father on weekends, when things like this cropped up, or when his friends told what they were planning to do with their fathers.

His father was a truck driver. Mick remembered him with tough, tattooed arms strong enough to swing a semi neatly around in any small space. He remembered him eating huge dinners in the evening, doing his football pools, drinking beer from cans, and going out with his friends—never with Mama, only with his friends.

One day, he drove off as though it was any ordinary day, but it wasn't so ordinary, because he didn't come back. Mama was ill for weeks after that. She didn't know where he was. But he had taken his best clothes with him, so *he* had known where he was going. *He* knew where he was now, but they didn't. They never spoke about him anymore, and Mick tried not to look at his chair, the one with the yellow stretch cover.

"Yes, what do we need, Mick?" Mama was asking.

"Er—we need—we need chipboard, I suppose, or some stuff like we have in school."

"Chipboard, if you say so. And what else?"

"Screws—nails—and a couple of pieces of wood to fix the board firmly to the wall."

"Right. We'll go and see what we can get," said Mama.

"Honestly? Can we? Wow!" cried Angelo, scrambling out into the open. "That's great."

"I want to go to the market anyway, so we'll stop at that little do-it-yourself shop there and see if they've got the board."

Mick put his pencils away, then took one of them out again. "I'll measure the wall," he volunteered. Taking his ruler, he went into the bedroom. There was only one narrow wall alongside the door that they could use.

"Don't forget, Mick, measure in meters, not yards," Mama called.

"What else!" Mick smiled and then muttered to himself, "The boy millimetered his way in from the meter on his two tired centimeters, to measure the wall with his meter stick."

Maybe today wasn't going to be just another long Saturday after all. . . .

5

Fish and Chipboard

The market on Saturday was a jungle of hot, fussy people pushing their way between stalls. Mick didn't think Mama enjoyed it much. She never looked happy there. He suspected she only came to the market on Saturdays to give them something to do. It took care of Saturday morning between cleaning the apartment and having lunch. If the weather was good in the afternoon, they sometimes went to the park with a football. That took care of the afternoon. In the evening, they watched television or played games of Scrabble, Battleships, and Monopoly.

Rain made one Saturday seem as long as three

put together, and Mama's face would look strained as the hours dragged by. Wrestling with Ange was fun and Mama didn't mind it, but it never lasted long. Ange would fall off the bed or squeal, and that would bring Logie-the-bogey out onto the stairs, banging and shouting like an angry troll.

"Ssssh, or he'll tell us to leave," Mama would say. "Better play something quiet. You have to be quiet."

Sometimes Mick dreamt about standing in the middle of a big field and opening his mouth and *shouting*. Shouting for the sake of making the noise that was never allowed to come out of him. He couldn't keep it shut inside himself forever. At school he was naturally quiet, but there were times when he wanted to be naturally noisy. . . .

"Well, Mick, got the measurements with you?" Mama asked when they arrived at the little do-it-yourself shop under the railway bridge. Stacks of boards were piled high on the pavement against the storefront, together with gates, moldings, and trellises.

"Where's the chipboard? Can you see any chipboard?" Mama knew nothing about such things, so Mick took over and did the shopping. He found a piece of board that was the right width and nearly the right length—only eight centimeters short of a square. He chose two slats of wood from a box, and a pack of nails from a display stand.

"It doesn't matter about the board being short, Mama," he said. "Eight centimeters, that's nothing. I've got everything. What d'you think?" He was anxious to get home and start work. This would be the biggest thing they had tackled together.

When Mama saw the price of the board, she opened her purse and counted through her bills before saying, "That's all right. Yes, we'll take it." She used nearly all the money she had with her.

"How do we carry it?" asked Angelo.

"That's a good question," Mama said. "We'll have to walk home with it. This won't go on a bus." She tried to hold the chipboard under her arm, but it was too wide to grasp at the bottom.

"Best on the boys' heads," said the man who had taken their money. "Most people manage these on their heads. You try."

Between them they hoisted the rectangular board onto Mick's head; Angelo supported it behind. And with Mama calling out. "Excuse me! Excuse me, please!" they negotiated the edge of the market and turned onto the street that led home.

"I feel stupid. Everybody's looking at me," said Mick.

"Nonsense," replied Mama. "Nobody's taking the slightest notice. Why should they? We're carrying a piece of chipboard, that's all."

"I can't see where I'm going," complained Angelo.

"Just watch Mick's feet and it will be all right," Mama said. But she walked behind, now and again easing the board up a little so Angelo could peer out to the side.

They hadn't gone much farther when Mick heard, "Hey, hey, that's some parade you got there, man."

Napoleon Leroy swerved to a stop at the curb on his luminous green International Super bike. In his left hand he held a crumpled newspaper package that steamed and smelled of vinegar.

"Hi, Leon."

"You're going to hurt yourself, kiddo," Leon said. "Gimme, gimme, gimme here." He flipped his bicycle up on the sidewalk and insisted that they put the chipboard across the seat and handlebars.

"That's very kind of you, Leon," said Mama. "I'll take this for you. Is it your lunch?"

"Yeah. My folks are at a wedding. Have a chip, Mrs. Tooley. They're still hot."

"No thanks, Leon, but that's an idea. What about it, boys?"

"Yes, fish and chips for lunch! I'd like that," said Mick, brightening up.

"Well, fish anyway," said Mama. "I can make chips at home. I've got plenty of potatoes."

"Oh, Mama, they're not the same," called Angelo, who was trailing behind, rubbing his arms. "Can't we have chips from the shop, just for once? They taste different in newspaper."

Mama smiled and said she'd buy them—just for once, to please them. By this time they had come to the fish shop where Leon had been. "You go ahead," said Mama. "Don't stop with that thing. I'll catch up."

So they walked on with the chipboard resting on Leon's bike, and Angelo attracting everyone's attention by hopping about and shouting, "Fish and chipboard. Que-e-e-e-eh! Fish and chipboard. Que-e-e-e-eh!"

"Is he nuts?" asked Leon, laughing.

"Completely," replied Mick. "That's his main problem."

6

Leave It to Napoleon

By the time Mama caught up, carrying two steamy packages in her shopping bag, Mick had explained to Leon what the chipboard was for.

"I'll give you a hand if you like," Leon said. "I don't have to be home until six. Uncle Sam does this kind of thing. Sometimes I help."

"He's handy, your uncle," said Mick.

"Oh sure, he can do anything worth doing." Leon sounded proud of his Uncle Sam. "Back in Jamaica he had his own fix-it business, called Uncle Sam's. He took in most things that needed repair. Just Uncle Sam's. Everybody knew him back there."

When they got home, they opened the packages and ate their lunch right out of the greaseproof paper. Mama laughed and let them get on with it.

"I think we'll do this more often," Mama said gaily. "It saves me washing dishes." She thrust her hand into the paper among the other snatching fingers. At once Angelo caught hold of one of her fingers.

"Ooops! Sorry about that. Thought it was a chip!" he screeched. "They taste better out of newspaper, don't they, Mama?"

"Well—maybe there's something to be said for hot newsprint. But I'm not sure what," countered Mama, winking.

Her cheeks were pink and her eyes shone. There were lots of little reflections in her eyes that weren't usually there. She was quiet and gentle, but she was not at all pretty, Mick thought. Nobody could call Mama *pretty*. . . . He remembered the day he'd come home from school with a split lip. When Mama asked about it, he told her he'd walked into a door. It was the only lie he recalled ever telling his mother. But he couldn't have told the truth. He could never have said that Joey McColgan had called her Concorde. Maybe her nose *was* long and pointed, but she was his mother. And, *Concorde*!

So, he'd punched Joey, and Joey had hit back with his football cleats in a plastic bag. That was how his lip had been split. But it had been well worth it.

When they had finished the fish and chips and a plateful of bread and butter, the boys were ready to start work. Mama tied on her apron and examined the chipboard as though it was an unidentified object. Mick smiled.

"Mama, why don't you sit down and put your feet up? You could read the paper. Relax, and don't look until we call you. We'll give you a surprise." He took her to the sofa and spread out the cushions. "Will you?"

"If you say so. I'd like that," said Mama. She slipped off her shoes and swung her legs up on the sofa.

Mick knew Mama would be surprised if he managed to get the bulletin board up. Carpentry was not his strong point, any more than it had been his father's. But she picked up the paper and seemed to forget about the bulletin board right away. *I'll bet she's pretending,* thought Mick.

"What can I do to help, Mick? What can I do?" cried Angelo, hopping up and down in excitement. Mick groaned inwardly.

Leon said quickly, "Listen, Ange, me and Mick,

can put this up for you—uh, kind of like a surprise. Okay? Then when it's done, you can pin up all your pictures."

To Mick's amazement, Ange said, "Well, all right. And I'll pick out my best pictures."

"Sure, good man. Come on, Mick, let's get going."

It wasn't long before Mick knew he had problems. He didn't remember how hard it was to hammer a nail straight and true. "How is it your nails go in straight, Leon? Mine bend—just look at them." Mick pointed to a small heap of miniature horseshoe shapes. "I won't have enough nails if I don't get the hang of it."

"It's knack, pure knack, man—and with an uncle like mine, how could I go wrong? You know Ernie's corner store, by the apartments?"

"Uh-huh."

"Uncle Sam put up all the shelves in there. And he fitted a new door. I helped with the door."

"Wow, Leon!" said Angelo. He was sitting on the floor outside the bedroom, sorting his pictures. "You're going to be a carpenter when you grow up!"

"Whaddya mean, 'going to be'? I am. I am." Leon beat his chest proudly.

At that moment, the doorbell rang.

"Milkman," called Mama.

"Don't move, Mama! I'll get it." Mick dropped his hammer. He was glad to have an excuse to get away from the embarrassing pile of bent nails. "I'll leave it you, Leon," he said.

"Yeah, yeah! You do that. Leave it to Napoleon, he's happy." He had already nailed the two supporting slats to the wall.

Mama held out her purse. "Get an extra pint. I'll make some hot chocolate for the workmen." She had a tray across her knees. On it was a half-finished jigsaw puzzle of the Battle of Waterloo. "Some relaxation," murmured Mick. The bell rang again.

Mick leapt down the staircase. At the bottom, Logie-the-bogey was drying his bald head with a towel. "Come on, come on! He's wasting my battery," he whined. "Can't get a minute's peace for a shampoo. And what's the ruckus up there?"

Mick didn't reply at once. He opened the door and paid the milkman. Then he went out with him to get the extra pint from the milk truck parked at the bottom of the hill. When he came back, he closed the front door slowly and gently, without making a sound. But Mr. Logie was still there.

"I *said,* what's the ruckus up there today?" He jerked his thumb upward.

"That, Mr. Logie, is Napoleon," Mick said clearly.

"Who?"

"Napoleon."

"What are you talking about?"

"Napoleon. Remember? He escaped from Elba—on a luminous green International Super bike. Well, he's parked it over there." Mick didn't give a flicker of a smile. He nodded to the corner of the hall where Leon's bike stood half hidden by a coat-tree. Then he fled up the stairs.

On the first landing, he paused and looked over the banister. Logie-the-bogey was stooping over the bicycle. *Checking the historical facts,* thought Mick.

When he reached the apartment, Mick couldn't believe his eyes. The bulletin board was up. It was on the wall. Leon and Ange were putting in the final nails.

"Surprise, Mick!" called Angelo, waving his hammer. "How about that?"

"How did you do it so fast?" Mick asked. He stood in the doorway, amazed.

"No problem, man," said Leon with a wide, pearly smile. "That's not wall you got there, it's only paneling. Plasterboard, I think. If that was real wall, we'd have needed your dad's electric drill. But this—kid stuff. Ange did it with me."

"Oh," said Mick. So Ange could hit a nail straight too. Only *he* couldn't. "That's great. Thanks, Leon. Thanks, Ange." He was glad his dad's electric drill hadn't been asked for. He had neither dad nor drill. Dad had never been a handyman.

"Mama, it's ready!" shouted Angelo.

"Coming!" called Mama. "I'm just finishing off Waterloo. Hang on—I've—I've done it."

She padded into the bedroom without her shoes and clasped her hands with pleasure. "Marvelous! I can't believe it. That was worth all the effort, wasn't it? It deserves a cup of hot chocolate all round!"

Shortly before six o'clock Leon said, "See you," and was gone. He went so fast, it was hard to imagine he had been there at all. But the bulletin board was firmly fixed to the wall to prove it.

"He's a really nice boy, that Napoleon," said Mama. They watched him through the window as he pedaled off, standing up and zigzagging to gather speed. "He's really nice."

Mick nodded. He knew that every time his eyes turned to that bulletin board he would see Leon's brown shiny eager face. "Mm, he's kind," he muttered.

And he realized what a short Saturday it had been. The shortest on record. A real record-breaking Saturday.

7

"Four Vests, Angelo!"

The Sunday routine never varied. Mama always made a cooked breakfast, and they took time to enjoy it in their pajamas. They each had bacon and eggs and lots of fried bread cut in triangles. The geometry of the bread was important. Square slices were never the same, just as homemade chips were never the same as chips out of newspaper.

Sunday breakfast was the kind of breakfast Dad had liked best of all. Mick wondered if Mama cooked it in the hope that one Sunday morning Dad would walk in and take his usual place at the table. She never said so. Mick didn't even know if she was sad anymore. Sometimes people asked about Dad when they were out shopping, and Mama would say, "Oh, he's always on the road. His job takes him to the Continent, you know. The whole of Europe's in easy reach nowadays, isn't it?" The rest was covered up.

After Sunday breakfast, Mama would read the paper before she got dressed. It was one luxury she allowed herself. Mick and Angelo mostly argued about who should be the first to read the weekly *Look and Learn* magazine. The argument had become a habit; now it seemed almost more important than the magazine itself. Mama had twice threatened to cancel the subscription.

"Why *do* you argue?" she would say in exasperation, putting her paper down. "When you go to bed tonight, will it matter who read the magazine at ten and who read it at two? It's not important."

She had a way of breaking things down into sensible, logical pieces, the way Mr. Rivers could break down fractions in math class. A candy bar always came into Mick's mind during such arguments. It was a candy bar Mama had brought them once. She hadn't cut it exactly down the middle, and they had come to blows over it. Mama had intervened, saying, "Eat it, and after you've swallowed your piece, tell me how and where it matters who had the extra millimeter. Do you feel it in your stomach, in your mouth, in your arm? *Where* has it made any difference? It's only in your quarrelsome little minds."

And Mama had settled all their arguments over candy bars in a clever way. She had said, "In future, one of *you* will cut it in half, and the other one will pick the piece he wants."

Mick knew Mama was right about these things. But irritation with Ange often got the better of him, and he wound up arguing anyway.

By the time Mama had read the paper, it was time for church.

"All right, into your suits, boys, it's a quarter to twelve," Mama would say, clapping her hands.

This Sunday, Angelo asked, "Can I go in my jeans, Mama? They're clean."

"Never! Don't even suggest it."

Suddenly Ange was filled with a burning interest in the magazine Mick was reading. They sat side by side, friends for the moment, as Mick leafed through the *Look and Learn*—an old copy. Anything was better than squeezing into suits, white shirts, and ties. "Come on, Ange," Mick said finally, putting down the story of Prince Vlad of Rumania and his cruel ways. "We'd better get ready. . . . He really was Dracula, you know, Prince Vlad."

"Wow! He put people's heads on sticks, didn't he? And he nailed people's hats to their heads. I saw it in a book. Oooooh, Dracula!" gasped Angelo, taking a last look at the illustration of Prince Vlad with fangs. "Read it to me when we get back, Mick."

"Why should I? You've got the new mag. This one's last March. You can read it yourself when I've finished," said Mick.

"But I can't read all the words yet. I want to hear about Dracula, Mick," Angelo pleaded.

"Tough luck!"

"Oh, Mick! I'd do it for you, if you were my age."

"Shut up."

"You're always telling me to shut up. Why do I always have to shut up?"

"Because you *don't,* that's why." Mick carefully put his pencil case on top of the *Look and Learn* and left it on a chair, reserving it for later. "Don't you dare touch that," he warned, and he went to get his white shirt from the closet.

Mama had her red dress and her white beret on before either of the boys had buttoned up his shirt.

"Can we take the bus, Mama?" Mick asked, tugging at his collar as though he was being strangled.

"Bus? What bus? Try and find one on a Sunday. Anyway, the walk will do us good. There's a pleasant breeze."

43

"But it's raining," Mick protested, trying not to look at the dry window.

"It was. That was at nine o'clock. Polish your shoes, please. Angelo!" Mama raised her voice.

Mick got out the shine kit, as Angelo appeared in the doorway looking hot and bothered.

"What's wrong? Do you feel all right?" Mama asked.

"I'm hot." Angelo threw himself into a chair.

"Then you must have a fever. It's not a warm morning." Mama was about to go for the thermometer, but turned back quickly and stared as Angelo bent to put on his shoes. "What on earth . . . ?"

Angelo's shirt slid up as he bent over. There was a flash of white, red, blue, and yellow between his shirt and trousers. "What *have* you got on?"

"Clothes," replied Angelo. He stood up sharply, pulled his shirt down, and began to back out of the kitchen with one shoe in his hand. "Just clothes, that's all."

He had almost shuffled out of sight when Mama grabbed him by the arm. She yanked up his shirt. Beneath was an assortment of undershirts: white, red, blue, and yellow.

"For goodness sake, child, no wonder you're hot. Four vests, Angelo!"

"Well, I can't help it." He squirmed, but Mama held on fast. "I can't help it. The first one was back to front, the second one was inside-out, then I got my head through the armhole of the other one. But the yellow one's all right, honestly."

"But why didn't you take them off?" asked Mama.

"There wasn't time. You said to hurry, and I can't get my head out of the armhole anyway." Beads of perspiration stood on his face, and his curls stuck damply to his forehead. "Well, I can't help it!" he said, throwing out his arms helplessly.

He was ready to cram all this bulk into the jacket of his suit, but Mama would not allow it.

"Get the vests off."

"But I can't. My head—it's the armhole—"

"Get them *off*, I said. You're not going into God's house in four vests."

"He won't see them," persisted Angelo.

Mick smiled. "God knows and sees all things, even our most secret vests." He laughed, as much at his own joke as at Ange's antics. Ange was only really funny when he didn't mean to be.

Mick could see that Mama was trying not to laugh. After all, they were going to be late for church, and that was a serious matter.

The vests problem proved to be serious too. Mama tried to pull all four off at once, to save time, but they wouldn't come.

"Ow! You're pulling my head off. Ow, watch

it! My head!" yelled Angelo, his face red and very moist.

"You're a tiresome little boy!" Mama scolded. She couldn't get his head back through the armhole of the blue one. "You've got your head *and* your arm through the same hole. How did you manage it? No—don't tell me. We'll get in after the sermon at this rate. Oh, Angelo!"

"We could dial 911 and get a fire truck to come over," suggested Mick. "Like you would if he'd stuck his head in the railings." He tried to imagine what Mama would say: "Operator, get me the firehouse quickly. My son's got his head stuck in his vest."

The emergency was soon over—Mama, in desperation, took the scissors and cut across the shoulder of the blue vest. "What a thing to do to a good vest! I'll see if I can mend it later. Now hurry, Angelo, hurry," she urged, flinging the extra vests on the sofa.

They took a bus after all. A red bus shape came rolling into view in the distance as they turned into the High Street, so they sprinted to the stop. Within minutes they were walking into the dim light of the church.

Mick went ahead to join the choir near the altar, where the choirmaster waited by the little organ. Angelo sat with Mama. She wanted him to. Granny

46

Mia had always said that families should sit together in church at least once a week. What Mama didn't know was that some of the time Angelo knelt with his hands together, watching the priest at the altar, but *most* of the time he was crossing his eyes and sticking his tongue out between his fingers for the benefit of anyone in the choir who happened to be looking.

When the service was over, Mick knew, Angelo's fingers would creep along the bench towards Mama's arm and tap it. She always gave him money to light a candle at one of the shrines. Granny Mia used to keep the church illuminated with her candles.

Mick watched. Angelo rose and went to the shrine of Saint Anthony and dropped the money into the metal box. He took a white candle and lit it from one already burning. Reaching up, he wedged his candle firmly into a holder close to the statue.

Mick watched. Ange's legs were like two twigs in kneesocks. The legs of his knee pants seemed too wide for him, and creased upward at the front. Mick felt a pang of sorrow that he wasn't kind to Ange. He knew he wasn't kind. Too often he couldn't be bothered with his young brother and found no real pleasure in his company. He resented the way Ange followed him everywhere, resented having to look after him. But he had regrets in church when Ange looked so skinny, as if he could be broken like a twig. "Poor skinny thing," he murmured. If Ange had turned and looked at him at the moment, he could have shown his feelings in a smile that said, "You're my little brother and here's my special smile for you." But Ange didn't turn around—he was busy.

As Angelo and Saint Anthony went on looking at each other, Mick wondered about the candles. Did Mama want Saint Anthony to help find Dad? He was, after all, the special saint who helped you find things. Or did she want him to help her find a way of managing *without* Dad? You could never tell with grown-ups. They hid so much. Sometimes you found answers in their eyes, not in their words. Mama's eyes were on Ange.

"I'll read him Prince Vlad of Rumania when we get home," Mick mumbled into the hymnbooks he was collecting.

After lunch, they quarreled about who should clean up pencil shavings from the rug. "They're yours," snapped Mick.

"No, they're not! I didn't use brown or yellow, so they can't be mine," Angelo snapped back.

In the end, Mama made them do it together, and they trod on each other's fingers and exchanged a few concealed punches.

"I don't know why you go to church," Mama sighed. "If it does you any good, it certainly doesn't show. Now let's have a game of Scrabble."

"But I can't spell—" began Angelo.

"I'll help you, as I always do," Mama said patiently.

Under his breath, Mick jeered, "Little baby Tooley!"

The gold of the candles, thin vulnerable Angelo, and reading aloud about Prince Vlad of Rumania were already forgotten.

8

The Sand Pencil

"Have you got the lunch money, Mick?" Mama asked on Monday morning.

"Yes, and I've got the honey for the Christmas bazaar, and Kleenexes." Mick patted his bookbag and gave his mother a quick kiss.

"And I've got my what's-it and my other what's-it, and my what's-it's what's-it," beamed Angelo, raising his face for a good-bye kiss.

Mama took the face between her hands, deposited a kiss, and ruffled Angelo's springy curls.

"Come on, nut-case," growled Mick. He started

off down Nightingale Rise with Angelo trotting behind him.

Mama gave them a wave before they turned into
the High Street, then hurried in to get ready for
work.

Mick always liked Monday mornings. He liked
thinking about the week ahead, and considering
how he could do things to please Mr. Rivers.

Sometimes he found himself thinking of Mr. Rivers as his father: Mr. Rivers taking them all shopping
in his car, or to see a film; playing football in the
park with Mr. Rivers, with Mama watching, instead
of trying to kick the ball in her sandals; Mr. Rivers
making Mama laugh until her cheeks turned pink.
The idea appealed to him. . . .

Mr. Rivers cared about people. He was always
interested in anything that anyone had to say. He
looked at you with his blue eyes magnified by his
glasses and made you believe you were saying something really important. Even if you only said, "I've
lost my shorts, sir," he would look at you as if
you'd given him a world news flash.

Mick's spirits always soared during math class.
He liked math. He enjoyed taking numbers and
juggling them, making them increase or disappear,
giving them names like "x" and "y." "Michael's
got the hang of it. Come on, the rest of you," Mr.
Rivers would call out, rubbing his hands together

when Mick was the only one to thrust his arm up, volunteering the correct answer. "Look out, Einstein, here he comes!" he would boom when Mick gave the answer to a difficult problem.

Mick spent the morning break cleaning up the stockroom with his teacher. "Well, it's your last year here at Saint Mary's, Michael," said Mr. Rivers. "Angelo will miss you next year."

"He'll manage, sir," Mick replied quietly as he stacked a pile of decrepit-looking textbooks. He was thinking, *I'll miss you.* Then he said, "Are these to go in the bin?"

"No, no. I have to account for them on the stock list. Thank goodness the new ones can be sponged clean. These are disgusting. If you give me a hand during afternoon break, we'll get this job finished."

"Yes, sir! I'd like to," said Mick as the whistle blew for the end of break.

Napoleon Leroy went home to lunch, so it was not until the end of the day that Mick had a chance to talk to him.

"The board's still up," Mick said as they left the classroom together.

"Whaddya mean, *still up!* What did you expect?" Leon jerked back a couple of steps in mock offense. "That's there for keeps, man, unless the wall falls down."

"Well, I didn't mean to—"

"Here, Mick. I brought it for you. Here y'are."

Leon took a sand pencil from his pocket. It was exactly like the one he had shown Mick on Friday.

"Oh, you remembered!" Mick said. "Thanks a million, Leon. You're sure you really want to give it to me?"

"Sure I'm sure. It's yours, Mick."

"I should be giving *you* something for helping on Saturday." Mick suddenly felt at a loss to match Leon's generosity. "Have a Kleenex, or a shoelace?" he joked, lifting one foot.

"Go on! Where's Ange?"

"He's somewhere—worse luck."

"Come on, Mick. You're too hard on him. . . . I wish I had a pencil for him, but that's my only extra one. Oh, there he is—ouch!"

There was a flurry of arms and legs, and a "Que-e-e-e-eh" screeched out of the cloakroom. Angelo had been lying in wait for them.

Mick scowled and made a wide arc around the flying figure, but Leon roared with laughter. "Hey, man, you'll grow feathers if you keep that up."

"I already have," squawked Angelo. He dived into his bookbag and produced two long white feathers, which he held against the seat of his pants.

Mick showed no interest, but Leon said immediately, "Swans?"

"Yes. Dicky Evans went to Henley* on Sunday. He found them on the riverbank. They're royal." Angelo stuck the feathers behind his ears.

"Want a piggyback ride?" Leon bent over, and Angelo leapt up and clung to his neck.

"Giddy-up! Giddy-up!" Ange shouted, and his voice echoed along the corridor.

"You going to your uncle's again?" Mick asked as they turned out of the school gate together.

"No. I'm taking my sister to the dentist for a filling. Here's Francie."

A small dark girl in a white blouse joined them silently. She smiled, keeping her face shyly close to Leon's sleeve. With his left hand, Leon expertly buttoned up her coat. Angelo made a face at her and she giggled, but said nothing.

As they moved away from the school, Mick gazed at the sand pencil, turning it over in his hand. He would put it on his dresser, together with the two postcards showing pictures of Rome (where Granny Mia had come from), and the three frogs made of shells he'd bought at a school rummage sale.

"How do they get the sand in like that?" asked Angelo, peering over Leon's shoulder at the pencil.

* Borough west of London, scene of annual rowing race, or regatta.

"Pour it in, stupid," muttered Mick, annoyed that his thoughts had been interrupted.

"Yes, but how does it stay in the same place, in stripes, I mean?"

"It's tightly packed," Mick said curtly.

He didn't want Ange to go on asking questions. He was *always* asking questions. "Leon," he said, "what about—"

"Yes, but I mean—" Ange said at the same time.

"Shut up!"

"I only want to know—"

"Shut *up!*"

"Yes, but—"

"Will you *shut up!*" said Mick angrily. "I'm trying to talk."

"Oh, shut up yourself!" retorted Angelo, in a rare flash of anger. "Shut up! Shut up! Shut up! It's *always* shut up, with you. Shut up yourself for a change!"

He thrust out with one foot and kicked Mick's arm. It wasn't a hard blow, but it was sudden and unexpected.

In his surprise, Mick let the sand pencil slip from his fingers. It fell at such an angle that the plastic tube split. In a moment the sand had poured out. Silently the colors ran into each other, forming a tiny heap of sand on the road. The special Isle of Wight stripes were gone.

They stopped and stared. Mick couldn't believe his eyes. It had happened so fast. His present from Leon was there in his hand, and then it wasn't. The special Isle of Wight pencil was now nothing more than an ordinary writing pencil, painted brown—and a short one at that. It seemed an eternity before Mick could bring himself to stoop and pick it up, leaving the sand behind.

Leon pushed his mouth out into a disappointed pout. "So what," he drawled. "We'll get more next year. The Isle of Wight's still there." His sister clung more tightly to his sleeve and hid her face.

Angelo slid to the ground, pale and frightened. "I didn't mean to. Honest, Mick, I didn't," he half shouted. "I didn't do it on purpose!"

"You pig! You miserable little *pig!*" Mick exploded. "I've had enough of you. I've had enough." He lunged forward, but Angelo ducked out of the way.

"Hey, hey, man! Hold it!" said Leon, grasping Mick's arm.

"He's a creep. I've had enough of him." Mick's face was red now, and he was shouting. "He ruins everything. Why do you have to be around all the time, trailing after me? I'm fed up with you. Why did you have to be born? Get out of here! Go on, get lost. You can find your own way home. Rotten pig!"

A small crowd of children had gathered at the sound of the commotion. Mick only half noticed them. He was wild with rage and distress at the loss of his present from Leon.

Angelo said no more. He backed away, his eyes round with shock. He fell against the bumper of a parked car; then, picking himself up, he turned and began to run.

Tears filled his eyes and splashed down his gray school sweater. He bolted blindly, like a panicking animal.

Angelo ran on between the parked cars, on past the apartments where Leon's uncle lived. As he turned toward the shortcut through the park, he slowed down. There were three German shepherds running loose. A man was with them, but the dogs were enormous, like three hungry wolves. Angelo's legs trembled as he lost speed. With a backward glance at the dogs he swerved away from the gate. He ran on down the road to take the long way home along the High Street.

9

911

Leon tried to calm Mick down.

"Don't be so upset, man. What's eating you? It's only a pencil. It's not important."

They were walking by the apartments now. Francie, who had been frightened by the shouting, was whimpering and holding tightly to her brother's hand.

"It *is* important. You sound like my mother. And it's not one thing. It's lots of things, *months* of things. Why did he have to go and do that? He kicked me on the arm with his foot. You saw him."

"Well, maybe it was *my* fault," said Leon softly.

"If I hadn't given Ange a piggyback ride his feet would have been on the ground, and if you'd put the pencil in your pocket, it wouldn't have happened. We can all blame each other, but for Pete's sake—it's only a pencil."

"I know, but—"

"But nothing! Come on, Mick, you'd better find Angelo. He's upset."

"He's upset! Huh!"

They reached the park. Dusk was settling quickly over everything, covering up the colors of the day. A light drizzle touched their faces. Mick looked across the wide expanse of grass, which was dotted with children hurrying home by the shortcut. Three German shepherds were happily chasing a ball. But there was no sign of Angelo.

Mick said, "He'll be home by now, waiting for me on the doorstep, if he ran all the way. I'll walk on down to the corner with you."

They walked silently the rest of the way, as far as the corner by the Co-op. The High Street was shiny and wet, reflecting car lights that had been turned on early.

Leon swung his sister's arm up and down light-heartedly. "No more crying, honey. You can't take that face to the dentist."

"Sorry about everything, Leon," Mick said self-consciously. "Thanks for the pencil anyway. See you."

"Forget it, man. See you."

Mick stood for a moment watching Leon and Francie as they turned right and walked hand in hand toward the dentist's office. *Why couldn't Ange be like Francie?* Mick wondered. But he knew the idea was silly as soon as it formed in his mind. Ange was a boy, not a girl, and Ange was Ange. What was it he'd heard in science class? Something about cells. We're made up of millions of cells, with cell walls, and cell sap, and cyto—cyto—something. And among all the millions of people on earth full of millions of cells, no two people are exactly alike. We're all different.

Ange was *very* different.

Mick put his hand in his pocket and rolled the Isle of Wight pencil between his thumb and forefinger. "He's a creep, just the same, no matter how his cells are arranged," he said aloud.

The rain was coming harder now. Mick turned up the collar of his blazer and started to jog, keeping his eyes firmly fixed on the pavement just ahead of his shoes. He went on hating Ange, not knowing how to look at him when he got home. "He can make his own tea and get his own sandwich," he grunted, jamming his teeth together until they hurt.

In the distance a siren sounded. The noise came rapidly closer, rending the air. An ambulance raced by, followed by a police car. Other vehicles moved out of the way to let them pass. "Somebody's dialed 911," murmured Mick. "Maybe Ange is stuck in his vest again."

As he was picturing the vest crisis of Sunday morning, with Mama trying to wrench all four off at once, Mick became aware of the sound of splashing feet beside him. Lank, wet hair sprang up in front of his face, and a breathy voice said, "Mick Tooley! It's—it's y-your brother up there. It's your b-brother. It's Angelo!"

"What? Where?" Mick said, not recognizing the speaker at first. It was a girl from his school.

"It's your *brother!* He's been killed! That's the ambulance going for him, but he's dead."

"What? He's WHAT?"

Mick didn't wait to hear the dreadful word again. He'd heard it clearly the first time. "Ange! Ange! Ange!" he whispered, and a shiver ran through his body. He started to run, weaving through the shoppers, thrusting them aside with his arm, his bookbag swinging out from his shoulder. "Angelo! Angelo!" he shouted, between breaths that came like gulps of water.

Up ahead, just beyond the newsstand, lights were flashing. There was a crowd on the pavement. A dark blue van was wedged across the sidewalk, its cab buried in the smashed window of the shoe-repair shop.

Mick forced his way through the people. "Ange! Ange!" he cried frantically. Then he stopped, numb with horror.

The first things he saw were his black Commando shoes, the ones he'd handed on to Ange. They lay on their sides, empty, soaking up the rain. Two thin legs protruded from under the van. Two thin legs like twigs in knee socks—twigs that were red with blood. The gray school knee pants, almost unrecognizable, were blackened with grime and torn to shreds. The rest of Angelo was under the van.

Mick threw himself forward. Maybe it wasn't Ange. Maybe it was somebody who looked like him. Anybody could buy black Commando shoes, and gray knee socks and knee pants. Then Mick knew the legs were his brother's. *No two people are exactly alike.* Those legs could belong to nobody but Ange.

Someone was restraining him. Mick struggled within the strong grasp and sobbed, "But I'm his brother! That's m-my little brother. That's A-A-Angelo. I want to see him. *Let me see him!*" He couldn't even see the legs any longer. The ambulance men were half under the van with a stretcher, wrapping

Angelo up in a red blanket. "Let me see him!" Mick screamed. "Let me!"

"Don't worry, you'll see him, son. He'll be all right," said the policeman kindly.

"But he's dead! He's dead!"

"Dead? Certainly not. He's badly injured, but he'll be all right, you wait and see." The policeman released his grip and looked at his notebook. "You must be Michael," he said.

Mick nodded.

"A Mr., Mr.—er, Logie says he knows you. He was passing when it happened. He's gone to get your mother. She'll be here in a minute." The policeman's voice was calm and steady—he sounded as though nothing could ever surprise him. It made Mick feel a bit calmer.

Other arms took over and supported Mick as the policeman went to his car. Nothing seemed real to Mick any longer. Time was jolting backward and forward. He was still in school, waiting to walk home with Ange. He had the sand pencil, and Ange was still with him. They were nearly home. They only had to go around the corner now into Nightingale Rise. He was sure he was almost safely home with Ange.

But he wasn't. The ambulance door closed, and the ambulance raced off with Ange in it in the direction of the hospital, siren wailing. Mick's mind gradually came around again to four o'clock on a rainy afternoon—November twenty-eighth. Glistening on the wet pavement was a darker patch which he knew was not rain.

All around him people were talking at once. "Poor little soul, and all on his own." "You'd expect it up near his school, those apartments, but not here on the pavement." "It's pedestrians that need crash helmets, isn't it?" "Little darling, he never knew what hit him."

Then Mick saw his mother. She was coming along the pavement from the bus stop, leaning on the arm of Logie-the-bogey.

Mama looked years older than when Mick had left her that morning. She couldn't speak. Just as at Granny Mia's funeral, her voice seemed to leave her. Her mouth made the shape of the letter "M," but there was no sound.

"Mama, Mama," said Mick in a whisper. She shook her head, and tears fell from her eyes. She threw her arms around Mick and patted his back.

"Come on, laddie, I'll take you home," said Mr. Logie. At least, it looked like Mr. Logie, but it didn't sound like him. Mick peered at his face to make sure. At that moment, a second police car drew in to the curb, and Mama was whisked away as quickly as Angelo had been. "She'll be back when she's seen to the wee fellow," Mr. Logie was saying.

65

"Come on now, we'll go home and wait for her."

Mick couldn't understand this Mr. Logie who took him home and sat him on the sofa. It was odd to see *his* hand touching the doorknob, *his* shape walking across the living room. And it was odder still to hear a warm, rich Scottish voice trying to soothe him, instead of the usual ill-tempered yelling. Was this really the troll who bawled up the staircase if they made a sound?

Mick just let everything happen. A hot drink came, and chocolate cookies from a strange tin with a picture of a bagpiper on it. Mick ate and drank without lifting his eyes from the rug. And as he sat there, unable to think clearly, it seemed to him that from miles away came the faint smell of toasted cheese.

When Mama came up the stairs, Mr. Logie took her wet coat and scarf and hung them up to dry in the bathroom.

"How's the wee one?" he asked in a low, tender voice.

"He—he's—oh, he's bandaged—all over," Mama sobbed. "He was on the sidewalk, you know. He wasn't in the street. He was dragged along under the van. Oh, it's—"

Mama put her hand into the plastic bag she had been holding all the time, and drew out a bundle of rags. She pressed them to her face as though they were made of the finest silk, and cried into their wetness. The rags were all that were left of Angelo's clothes. Mama cried loudly and put her head on her knees.

Kneeling beside her, Mick put his arm around her shoulders. "I'm sorry, Mama. I'm sorry," he said softly into her ear. He realized she hadn't said, "Where were you? I'm glad you weren't hurt, but were you with Angelo? *You* didn't come for me." He was sure she knew very well he had not been with Ange, in spite of all her warnings. But she didn't reproach him.

"Have a hot drink. It'll make you feel better," Mr. Logie said. He put a cup of tea on the table, and a plate piled up with slices of toasted cheese. "I think I've a wee bit of ginger cake left downstairs. I'll go and bring it up."

As Mr. Logie went off to find the ginger cake, Mick said, "Can we go to see Ange? Is he in a ward?"

Mama nodded. "Later, this evening. But I'm not sure if they'll let you in."

"They will," said Mick. "They've got to. I'll make them."

10

"I'm Sorry, Ange"

Later that evening, Mick and Mama went to the hospital. Mr. Logie wanted to accompany them on the bus, but Mama insisted that they would be all right. They hadn't far to go, and Mama knew Mr. Logie never went farther than the High Street. (He never took a vacation, and didn't seem to have any relatives.)

Mick followed Mama into the brightly lit hospital. They walked through seemingly endless corridors until they came to the children's ward. The doors were closed, and parents were waiting anxiously, clutching packages of books, playthings, and food.

"How do we find Ange?" asked Mick.

"I know where he is. I remember. It's bed number twenty-one."

A nurse came and propped the swing doors open. "Sorry to keep you waiting," she said softly. "We had an emergency."

It was the whiteness of everything that struck Mick first of all: the white ceiling, the white sheets, the little white faces anxious for someone to smile at, and the white parts of the nurses' uniforms, stiff as cake icing.

"There he is," said Mama. "See him?"

Mick followed Mama's gaze. "Where? I don't see him. Where is he?"

"Right there."

Mick's eyes settled on one larger mound of white. His legs slowed down. The mound was a figure completely wrapped in bandages. The left arm was bent outward like the letter "L." Even the head was covered all over. It was large with dressings, and looked from the side like an astronaut's helmet. Mick stopped at the foot of the bed. There was a space where the eyes should be. The eyes were there, but closed.

As Mama moved closer, the long dark lashes twitched and parted. Wider and wider the eyes opened, until they were the shape and the velvety brown of Ange's eyes. They rested on Mick for a moment; then they turned upward to look at the white, white ceiling. Mama leaned over.

"How are you, Angelo?"

Mick's eyes began to burn. They were stinging with tears. His throat went stiff trying to stop them, but he couldn't. He just stood there and cried, until he thought his throat would burst. Each time the tears overflowed, he could see, just briefly. There was a small space in the bandages for Ange to breathe through, and another little one for his mouth. It was to this last one that Mama was listening.

"Can he speak, Mama?"

"Well, he's trying. He says—he's all right."

Mick didn't think she could really hear much of anything, but maybe that was what she hoped Ange had said. Just then, the sister who had opened the doors came swishing over to the bed.

"Could I have a word with you, Mrs. Tooley? Just for a moment," she said brightly.

Mama drew herself away from Angelo, and Mick hesitantly took her place.

"Ange?" he whispered. "Ange?"

The head remained still, but the eyes turned to Mick. They narrowed slightly, as if Ange was smiling.

"I'm sorry, Ange. It was all my fault. Can you hear me? Can you?"

The eyes blinked quickly, and a kind of "s-s-s" sound reached Mick.

"I'm sorry. Oh, Ange, you're not a creep at all. I didn't mean it. You're not a creep, honestly. *I* am. I'm a real creep."

Angelo's eyes closed tightly. He was screwing them up and saying, "Oooh—oooh."

"Oooh?" repeated Mick. "Ooooh? Oh, two? Two creeps? We're both creeps? Yes, well—"

The eyes relaxed and opened. But before Mick could say any more, Mama came back and began stroking the arm in the splint.

"He's got a broken collarbone, and his left arm is broken below the elbow—the tibia bone," she said. "And he's got a leg fracture below the knee."

"What about his head, Mama?"

"It's badly cut, but thank God it'll be all right. Oh, it could have been so much worse," she said, lowering her voice. Then she leaned over Angelo again. "You'll be as right as ever you were, darling. It's just a matter of time, Angelo."

Angelo's chest heaved in a big sigh, and he began to cry. Tears welled to the edges of his eyes and rolled over into the surrounding bandages.

"Oh, my darling, don't cry. Everything's already on the way to getting better. Everybody's kind and good here, and we'll be in to see you every day. You only have to think about getting well and com-

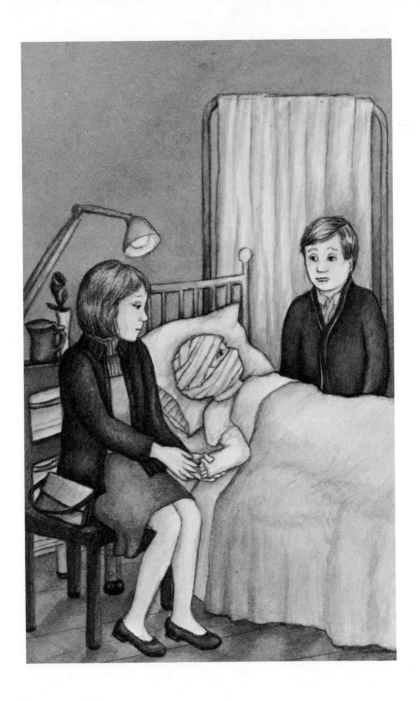

ing home. Mr. Logie sends you his love."

Angelo blinked. "Yes, he does," put in Mick, sensing Angelo's disbelief.

Mama smiled, and she and Mick between them went on to tell how kind Mr. Logie had been. Angelo's eyes shone through his pain. The time passed quickly. When the bell rang for the end of visiting hours, they suddenly found they had a great deal more to say. "We'll save it up for tomorrow, my darling," said Mama, trying to keep her voice low and firm. "Good night Angelo. God bless." She kissed his eyes and lightly touched the bandaged head where she would have ruffled his curls.

"Good night, Ange," said Mick.

"Mmmmmmmmm."

They were walking past the sister's desk when Mick suddenly turned and darted back. "Ange," he said. "I'll bring the *Look and Learn* tomorrow and read to you about Prince Vlad of Rumania— you know, Dracula. I'll read it as many times as you like. And, Ange," he added urgently. "I'll never *ever* tell you to shut up again. Never! I mean it. And I'm sorry for all the rotten things I've ever said, and for being mean to you. Believe me?"

Angelo looked straight at him, solemnly.

"D'you believe me, Ange? *Do* you? Come on, Ange! *Please!*" There was a silence so great that Mick felt the whole world was listening in. Then,

73

from behind the bandages, came a clear, long-drawn-out "Que-e-e-e-e-e-eh!"

Mick drew in his breath quickly and forked his fingers through his hair. His head began to fill up with "Que-e-e-e-ehs." It was as though Ange was saying it over and over again, louder and louder. It was the most endearing, most Ange-like sound he would ever hear. And Mick knew he would love it for the rest of his life.

His shoes squeaked on the polished floor as he turned and hurried to Mama, who was waiting patiently by the swing doors.

11

An Indelible Presence

As they sat on the bus going home, Mama twisted the tickets into shreds. Mick knew there was something she wanted to say.

"What is it, Mama?" he finally asked.

"Mick, oh Mick, do you know what they did to Angelo?"

"No. What did they do?" Mick shut his eyes tightly and said inwardly, *Please, God, not his feet or his toes. They didn't cut them off, did they?*

"They cut off his hair. *All* of it. The sister told me."

Mick let out his breath loudly, with relief. "Cut

75

off his hair? What did they do that for?"

Mama bit her lip. "Well, you know he was dragged along under the van, and he had nothing on his head. His head was on the ground, and— oh, all his curls. They're all gone. His poor, poor head." Mama turned her face away and looked out the window. Mick knew she wasn't really seeing anything outside.

He tried to imagine Ange without his curls. It wasn't possible. Nor was it possible to imagine how awful his head must feel. He'd only once cut his scalp on the school playground, and that had been bad enough. But a head full of cuts!

"Mama, his hair will grow back," Mick said gently. But she did not respond.

Mr. Logie was waiting for them at the front window. His bald head shone in the light from the streetlamp.

"How's the wee one? What did they say?" he asked as he opened the front door.

Mama told him all she knew as they walked up the stairs.

"He's a brave wee soldier, so he is," said Mr. Logie. "Now you take off your coats and come down to me. I've got your supper ready." Mama began to protest, but he put his finger to his lips. "Wheeeesht now. You come on down, and don't be long."

76

So Mama and Mick went down to the apartment where Mr. Logie lived. It was the first time they had ever been invited inside. It was like going into a glowing red cavern. Everywhere there was red tartan: on the fringed blankets covering the sofa and chairs, on the cushions—even the pictures on the walls were framed in tartan. And on a table in one corner, there was a set of bagpipes.

Mama looked astonished. "It's—it's very cozy," she said at last.

He made them comfortable at the table and, without any fuss at all, brought in trays of food. "Now, eat up, or I'll be sore offended," he said, handing out plates.

Mick couldn't remember afterward exactly what he had eaten, but he knew it had not come straight off a supermarket shelf. Mr. Logie could cook. And Mama must have enjoyed the meal, because in spite of her sorrow she ate everything she was given.

As Logie-the-bogey nimbly darted between them, offering dishes, coaxing them to eat, Mick felt he was in a magic world where the villain had been transformed. It was like the frog that became a prince, or the old crone who turned into a beautiful princess. And suddenly, Mick realized that transformations were not so farfetched. Here was Mr. Logie's bad temper turned to genuine affection. Magic

77

wasn't only for little kids. It could be a real part of everyday life.

Later, when Mick went to his room, the absence of Angelo hit him like a punch. If he didn't move, there was stillness. If he didn't speak, there was silence. Yet the stillness and silence held Ange's presence. His stamp was on everything. The bulletin board was crammed with his pictures of orange marshmen and purple swamp lizards, and a pair of underpants had been staked out with pushpins and labeled PANTING LUNAR MODULES. A book lay on his bunk, page 36 marked with a school sock. A tie was stuffed into the pencil jar on Ange's dresser, and a pink glass elephant carried on its back two of Ange's teeth that had recently come out.

Mick washed and put on his pajamas, but he couldn't bring himself to get into bed. He was standing looking at the bed when Mama came in. She hugged him and said tenderly, "Try to get some sleep, Mick, there's a good boy. You have to be up for school in the morning." Her long dark hair was loose and curled over the shoulders of her pink bathrobe.

"I won't be long, Mama," said Mick, twisting the loose curls. "Look, I'll come and say good night to *you* for a change, okay?"

Mama put her head on one side and smiled affectionately. Then she went out slowly, dragging her feet. Mick touched the bunk bed. He pushed it to make it creak. It wouldn't creak tonight, or the next night, or the next, or—Mick didn't want to think any further.

When he went to say good night to Mama, he thought at first she wasn't there. Her bed didn't look the right shape to have someone in it. But she *was* there, already asleep. Mick gazed at her. How lonely she looked, even in her sleep. She must be as lonely as he was. He would be without Ange only for a while, but Mama was alone every night. Whatever she did, she did alone. For the first time he began to understand Mama's quietness and weariness. It was like diving into a deep pool and surfacing with thoughts of the hidden things you'd seen.

Mick kissed Mama's forehead and tiptoed from the room, deep in thought. Mama didn't need to feel alone. She had him, and he had her, and they both had Ange. They were three Tooleys—not one and one and one, but a unit of three.

With these thoughts, Mick felt his need of Mr. Rivers diminishing. He no longer saw him as part of the family, playing ball, making Mama pink with laughter. He was outside the family, in his proper place at school, with the blackboard, the chalk, and the books.

Mick tightened the sash of his bathrobe and went

to the door to check it. It was already locked and bolted. He checked the windows. That was what Dad had always done. When he was satisfied that everything was in order, he turned out the lights.

Back in his bedroom, Mick picked up the book with the sock in it and tucked it under Ange's pillow. Then, climbing up, he slipped between the sheets to sleep in Ange's place. Lying in the dark, Mick slid his hand under the pillow until he grasped the sock. And, holding on to it, he sank into a dreamless sleep, knowing he was closer to his little brother that night than he had ever been since the day Ange was born.

12

Smokedrift to Heaven

The next morning, Mick didn't want to go to school. He wanted to go and see Ange in the afternoon. But Mama was firm:

"You must go to school, Mick. Every day's important. I'll see Angelo this afternoon, and we'll go together this evening."

Mick lingered over his breakfast, pushing his cereal around the top of his bowl. But when he saw that Mama wouldn't change her mind, he got up and collected his school things.

Before he left, he rushed into his bedroom and tipped all his money out of his red cigar tin. He didn't get much pocket money. Altogether he had fifty-nine pence. He counted out fifty-six, stuffed the money into his pocket, and buttoned up his blazer.

"Tell Ange I'm coming to see him tonight, will you?" he asked as Mama gave him his crackers to eat at break time.

"Yes, I'll tell him. And, Mick—" she added anxiously. "Take care."

Mick smiled. "Don't worry, Mama."

When he reached the turning that led off to the park and the shortcut to school, Mick stopped. He looked along the High Street. Just around the curve, beyond the fruit and vegetable store, was the shoe-repair shop. Mick felt an urge to go and see if the van had been towed away, to see if the shop had been boarded up, to see the place where it had all happened. Haltingly he went on along the High Street, remembering the darker patch that had glistened on the wet pavement. Then all at once he didn't want to go that way after all. He didn't want to see anything.

He turned abruptly, ran back to the corner, and took the shortcut across the park. He kept up a steady speed until he reached the apartments. At the curb he stopped, and, from habit, half turned to see how far behind Ange was.

As he came within sight of the wall around the school, he saw Napoleon Leroy. Mick could tell by his face that Leon knew about Ange. For once he wasn't smiling.

"Hi, Mick!" Leon said heartily as Mick came up. He planted a strong hand on Mick's shoulder and kept it there.

"Hi!" said Mick, looking at the sidewalk.

Leon put his hand into his blazer pocket and drew something out.

"Here, Mick. It's for you. Take it."

Mick glanced up. Leon was offering him a pencil. It was another sand pencil from the Isle of Wight.

"What?" he gasped. "Another one?"

"Sure! It's magic. Abraca-you-know. How many d'you want?"

Mick began to shake his head, but Leon stuck the pencil firmly in his top pocket. "Come on, man. It's for you. You take it? I'm happy. Okay?"

"No, I can't. It's your last one," Mick protested. Leon had *said* it was his last one.

"So, it's mine to give away, right?"

Mick looked into the brown face close to his. Leon's kindness amazed him. Mama's kindness amazed him. Mr. Logie's kindness amazed him. "Thanks," he said quietly. "You're great, Leon."

"Snuff it, Mick!" said Leon, giving him a bantam-weight punch on the arm.

Mick didn't go straight into school with Leon. "See you," he said hurriedly, and he went around to the front door of the church adjoining the school.

Three workmen were there building a new red brick wall around the forecourt. "Say one for me," one of them called out. Mick nodded and climbed the stone steps.

The church was silent and almost empty. An old man was moving from statue to statue, muttering and touching each one as though he was greeting old friends. Mick felt a nervous tingle in his arms and legs as he walked up the aisle to Saint Anthony's shrine. He drew the fifty-six pence from his pocket and dropped them into the metal box. Then, taking one candle after another, he lit twenty-eight—because the date of Ange's accident had been the twenty-eighth. As he stood there, bathed in a blaze of light, he saw the old man turn and smile at him. *Maybe he knows about Ange,* thought Mick.

Gently, gently, he blew on the candles, just enough to make the yellow flames bend over and flicker, forming little trails of smoke. Feathery, wispy traces wriggled upward. "Smokedrift," Mick murmured. And he followed the smoke with his eyes until it disappeared on its way to the rafters.

"Smokedrift to heaven, for Ange." He whispered his message, and blew an S.O.S. signal for good measure. It worked better than meat pie. "Let Angelo get better. Please, please," he went on. "I want him back in one piece. I'll look after him bet-

ter, honest!" And with no one to disturb him, Mick thought more deeply about Ange than he had ever thought about anybody, even Mama.

He thought of Ange standing in this same spot last Sunday. He thought of the smile Ange had never received from him. He thought of Prince Vlad and the reading he hadn't done. He thought of many other things. Reaching into his pocket, Mick drew out the precious sand pencil. This was for Ange too, he decided, because this present from Leon was what he most wanted to keep for himself. He would give it to Ange tonight, when he and Mama went to the hospital. When all three of them were together.

Mick walked down the wide middle aisle toward the church door. He felt taller than when he had come in, bigger and different in lots of ways. Mama and Ange didn't have Dad, but they had him. "The first-a man in your-a family." That's what Granny Mia had said.

He quickened his pace as he reached the shaft of daylight by the door. Then he leapt down the steps and vaulted over a section of the new red brick wall.

"Hey, you, get out of it!" hollered one of the workmen, raising his trowel in amusement.

Mick grinned and hurried into the yard as the school whistle blew.